Howie Bowles, Secret Agent

KATE BANKS

HOWIE BOWLES, Secret Agent

Pictures by ISAAC MILLMAN

Frances Foster Books

Farrar, Straus and Giroux   New York

Text copyright © 1999 by Kate Banks
Pictures copyright © 1999 by Isaac Millman
All rights reserved
Distributed in Canada by Douglas & McIntyre Ltd.
Printed in the United States of America
Designed by Rebecca A. Smith
First edition, 1999

Library of Congress Cataloging in Publication Data
Banks, Kate, 1960 –
    Howie Bowles, secret agent / Kate Banks; pictures by Isaac
Millman. — 1st ed.
        p.   cm.
    "Frances Foster books."
    Summary: Third-grader Howie Bowles copes with having to
change schools twice in one year by pretending to be a secret
agent named Agent Bean Burger.
    ISBN 0-374-33500-1
    [1. First day of school — Fiction. 2. Schools — Fiction. 3. Moving,
Household — Fiction.] I. Millman, Isaac, ill. II. Title.
    PZ7.B22594Ho   1999
    [Fic] — dc21   98-55144

For Hannah Bogardus—K.B.

Howie Bowles, Secret Agent

one

Howie rolled over in bed. He opened his eyes and looked at the ceiling. It looked strange. It was covered with stars. There were spaceships on the walls. Howie was wrapped in a sheet like a mummy. Where was he? Maybe he'd been kidnapped in his sleep and taken to another planet. Or another universe even. Howie sat up in bed. He heard footsteps. They were coming to get him.

"Yikes!" cried Howie. He dived under his pillow.

"Howie," called a voice. A familiar voice. It was his mother's voice. "Rise and shine."

Then Howie remembered. "Oh yeah," he said. This was his new room. In a new house. In a new place. Today he was going to a new school with a new teacher named Mrs. Beagle. Howie punched his pillow and tossed it on the floor. He might as well have been on another planet.

Howie's mom poked her head through the doorway. "How did you sleep?" she asked.

"Great," Howie lied. He'd had nightmares. He'd dreamed that his feet had started growing and didn't stop. But the rest of him stayed eight years old. It was scary. Really scary. But the scariest thing was that it *could* happen. That was the problem with life. Anything could happen. Like having your dad change jobs and having to change schools twice in one year. That had happened to Howie.

Howie untangled himself from the covers and rolled out of bed. What if he woke up

4

and his feet really were bigger than his body? Howie looked down. His feet looked pretty much the same. But when he put on his sneakers they felt a little tight. That worried Howie.

Lots of things worried Howie. Like sleeping by himself. Howie used to sleep with his little brother, Dylan. Dylan was three. Now Howie had his own room. He'd always wanted his own room. He'd always complained about Dylan. Dylan sucked his thumb. Dylan wet the bed. Dylan made strange noises in his sleep. Now Howie had his own room and suddenly he wished he was sleeping with Dylan. Life was like that, he guessed.

Howie put on his favorite T-shirt. It had a ketchup stain on the sleeve, courtesy of Ken Griffey, Jr. He'd dribbled it from a hot dog while signing autographs at a Seattle Mariners game. It was one of the most memorable days in Howie's life. Howie smiled when he thought of it. He smiled when he thought of baseball.

He loved baseball. Then he frowned. He wondered if anyone in his new school would love baseball. Would they even know what baseball was? Howie had seen a few kids on the block with skateboards or rollerblades, but no one with a baseball or a bat.

Howie sprinkled some food into his aquarium. "Frank, Felix, come and get it!" he said. Howie had two fish. There had been a third fish, but Frank ate it.

"It's a dog-eat-dog world," Howie's dad had said.

Howie thought about school. In third grade it could be a kid-eat-kid world. And Howie was worried that he might be eaten alive.

Howie went into the kitchen. His mother was mixing pancakes. Dylan was pouring milk from his cup into a saucer and lapping it up.

His mom dropped a postcard on Howie's plate. "Greetings from New York," she said. The postcard was from Howie's dad. He was away on business. He was always away on

business. Or at least it seemed that way to Howie.

Howie picked up the postcard. The front was a jumble of bright lights and tall buildings. On the back was a brief message. "Hi guys. Did you know that the Empire State Building has 6,500 windows? Miss you. Love Dad. P.S. Behave yourselves!"

Howie put the postcard down. No mention of school. No words of encouragement. Had his dad forgotten that Howie was about to begin life in a new school? That Dylan was going to real school for the first time? Howie shoved the postcard under his plate. What did he care how many windows the Empire State Building had?

Howie's mom hadn't forgotten about school. She'd left a new package of colored pencils, a block of paper, and a pad of Post-Its on the table for Howie. For Dylan there was a pack of fat, washable crayons and a glow-in-the-dark eraser.

"I'll bet you two are a little nervous," Howie's mother said.

Howie shrugged. He tore a Post-It from its pad and began scribbling. A new school. A new teacher. New kids. A new room. New books. "What's there to be nervous about?" he asked bravely.

two

Howie's seat was in the third row. It was kind of hard to miss. Mrs. Beagle had put a big sign on the back of his chair. "Howie, Welcome to room 7," it said. Howie sat down. The chair felt hard. He thought his desk was a little low.

"Today we have a new pupil," said Mrs. Beagle. Mrs. Beagle was young. Howie thought she looked too young to be a teacher. She looked nice, though. Not like one of those teachers who just waited around for you to make a mistake. Howie had had one of those at his last school.

Mrs. Beagle had orangy-red hair. Howie wondered if it was real. He wondered if she could have been born like that. Maybe it was a wig. Or maybe she'd put some stuff in her hair to change the color. Howie touched his own brown hair. He tried to imagine what he would look like as a redhead. Mrs. Beagle interrupted his thoughts.

"Let's everyone welcome Howie to room seven," she said.

Everyone looked at Howie. He felt like a bug under a microscope. He looked down at his feet and remembered his dream. Suddenly he started laughing. He couldn't help it. It was because he was nervous. He always laughed when he was nervous.

"What's so funny?" someone asked. Howie looked up. The girl sitting in front of him had turned around. She was the cutest girl he'd ever seen. She had blond hair with

ringlets and green eyes like a cat. And she had dimples.

"What's so funny?" she asked again.

"Oh, nothing," said Howie.

"My name's Maggie," said the girl. She smiled and Howie watched the dimples blossom in her cheeks.

He wasn't sure what to say. He could say his name was Howie, but that would be stupid. Everyone already knew that. It was written across the back of his chair and Mrs. Beagle had mentioned it a hundred times already.

"I know my multiplication tables up to seven," said Maggie.

Howie knew his up to ten, but he didn't want Maggie to think he was bragging. So he said the first thing that came into his head. "The Empire State Building has 6,500 windows."

"Oh," said Maggie. She didn't seem to care. She was staring at the stain on Howie's T-shirt.

"It's ketchup," said Howie. "Ken Griffey's ketchup."

"Who's Ken Griffey?" asked Maggie. She turned around and faced the front.

Howie was disappointed. Maggie didn't know who Ken Griffey was. Worse, she didn't want to know.

Howie thought about Maggie's dimples. He wished he had dimples. He sucked in his cheeks and stuck his finger in the little hollows. That's when the girl next to him kicked his chair. Her name was Mary Reilly. It was written on a piece of masking tape across the top of her desk. She had freckles and a big wide mouth that moved like an elastic band.

"You look funny," she said, and she wrinkled up her nose.

Howie relaxed his mouth. Mary Reilly made a face. Then she turned to Maggie. "Can I borrow your ruler?" she asked. Maggie handed Mary her ruler.

The rest of the morning was a daze. Howie

listened to Mrs. Beagle talking about numbers. Even numbers went anywhere. But odd numbers didn't fit. Howie closed his eyes. He felt like an odd number in a room full of evens. At his old school his teacher might have asked someone to show a new person around. Here, Howie was left to himself to figure out how to get from odd to even.

At recess Howie waited for someone to come up and say something to him. No one did. He watched his classmates play ball. There was Maggie, Mary Reilly, a boy with JUSTIN written across his sweatshirt, and another guy with a baseball cap. Mary Reilly always had to have the ball.

"Ball hog," said Howie under his breath.

"What did you say?" said Mary. She stood in front of Howie, hugging the ball.

"Polywog," said Howie. "There's a polywog in the puddle over there."

Mary Reilly twisted her mouth and wrinkled her nose. "You're weird," she said. Then she

tossed the ball to Justin and skipped off. Howie had brought some marbles but no one was playing marbles. Didn't anyone play marbles here? Howie looked around for Maggie. She was heading across the playground with Mary Reilly. They were holding hands. Howie thought that was strange. Girls were strange. They held hands and they whispered in each other's ears. Boys didn't do that.

Howie turned around. The guy with the baseball cap was leaning against the side of the school. He was eating a candy bar. His name was Toby Giles. He sat in the middle row, right in front of Mrs. Beagle's desk.

"Your name's Howie," he said. Howie nodded. He wasn't sure he wanted to be reminded of that again.

"I have six dollars and fifty-three cents in my pocket," said Toby. Howie reached into his pocket. He felt a dustball and a small hole.

Toby took another bite of his candy bar. Howie looked at his baseball cap. It was a Cardinals cap. He wondered if Toby knew who

Ken Griffey was. But he didn't ask. He didn't want to be disappointed. Maggie and Mary skipped back across the playground. Mary jumped in front of Toby.

"I can talk backwards," she said.

"Great," said Toby. "Can I have your autograph?" Howie laughed. He wished he'd said that.

"Fatty, fatty two-by-four," said Mary. Toby shrugged. He didn't seem to mind at all. But Howie did. He wanted to call Mary "volcano mouth." He'd heard that in a movie and thought it was funny. But he didn't dare. Howie looked at Maggie. She was tying her sneakers.

"My dog Dan-Boy has six toes," he said. He didn't know why he said it. But he thought it sounded good.

"Really?" said Maggie. She seemed interested.

Mary started laughing. Then she whispered something in Maggie's ear. Maggie laughed, too.

Howie wondered if they were laughing at Dan-Boy or at him. He felt confused. He didn't get it.

Mary held the ball in front of Howie. Howie didn't know whether to take it or not. "My mom's on the school board," said Mary.

Howie shrugged. "So what?" he said.

Mary tapped her foot. "She could get you kicked out of school," she said.

Howie wanted to say, "Big deal," but he didn't say anything. He didn't want to get kicked out of school. He turned to Toby. "Want to play tetherball?" he asked. He didn't think you could get kicked out of school for playing tetherball.

"Naw," said Toby. But he smiled. And it was a nice smile.

Howie walked over to the tetherball. He punched the ball. It sailed around the pole twice. Wham! Howie couldn't wait for the day to be over.

three

"Roll over," said Howie. "Ro-o-o-ll over." He held a dog biscuit high in the air. Dan-Boy opened his mouth wide and yawned. Then he dropped his head onto his paws and closed his eyes. It was useless. Dan-Boy wasn't interested in dog biscuits or in rolling over. He wasn't interested in being a dog. He was afraid of cats. And he didn't like to fetch. He just wanted to sleep and watch television.

"Oh, all right," said Howie. He flicked on the

TV and flipped to channel 5. Some lady was talking about books. That made Howie think of school. All those new faces. A room full of strangers. Howie didn't get it. When you were small, your parents were always telling you to stay away from strangers. Then when you got bigger they expected you to walk into a room full of strangers and be everyone's friend.

Howie went into the kitchen. Dylan had loaded up his dump truck with Dan-Boy's biscuits.

"*Vroom, vroom,*" he said. He pushed the truck under the table and emptied it. Then he picked up a dog biscuit and put it in his mouth.

"Dylan's eating dog biscuits again," Howie hollered. His mother was in the laundry room. She came down the hall with a pile of towels. Instead of scolding Dylan, she scolded Howie.

"You don't need to shout," she said sharply. She took the biscuit out of Dylan's mouth. "Those are for Dan-Boy," she explained.

"I'm a dog," said Dylan. He jumped up and nipped Howie's arm. "Bow-wow."

"No, you're not," said Howie loudly. Dylan started crying.

Mrs. Bowles picked up Dylan and swung him through the air. "I have an idea," she said. "Who wants to make bean burgers?"

"Bean burgers!" cried Dylan.

"Great," said Howie. Bean burgers were his favorite. He followed his mom into the kitchen. She set Dylan on a chair and tossed Howie an apron.

"You mix?" she said.

"Sure," said Howie.

"I want to mix," said Dylan.

"You can help," said Howie. He handed Dylan a wooden spoon.

His mom lined the ingredients up on the counter. She still hadn't asked about school.

Maybe she won't, thought Howie. But he knew better.

Suddenly his mother poked her head up

from inside the refrigerator. She set a package of cheese on the counter. "So tell me more about school," she said.

"School!" cried Dylan. Dylan had loved school. And he'd gotten a gold star for counting to ten.

"It's okay," said Howie. He took a fork from a drawer. "There's this girl Mary Reilly. She stinks." She didn't really stink. But Howie felt like saying that.

"Stinks?" said Howie's mom. "What does she stink of?"

"She has a big mouth," explained Howie.

Howie's mom nodded. "Oh, I get it," she said. "You mean, she's a know-it-all?"

Howie nodded. "Yeah," he said.

Howie's mom poured some bread crumbs onto a plate. "Did you make any new friends?" she asked.

Howie shrugged. He hadn't made any new friends. It was hard to make friends. Especially when everyone thought you were weird.

Howie's mother handed Howie an onion. She patted him on the back. "Don't worry," she said, smiling. "Just be yourself."

Howie began peeling the onion. Don't worry and just be yourself, he thought. What kind of advice was that? Howie was a worrier. He worried all the time. And why would he want to be himself? Wouldn't it just be easier to be someone else?

That night Howie had a hard time falling asleep. He tossed and turned.

"Don't worry," he told himself. "Just be yourself." Howie tried not to worry. But he worried that he wasn't trying hard enough. He turned on the light, reached for his new Detective Dare Brain magazine, and began reading. Detective Dare Brain was a secret agent known for his bravery and amazing memory. That's how he solved all his cases. He never used a gun. Howie flipped through the pages, until finally he fell asleep. He dreamed

he was a secret agent. He was on a case. He was trying to discover who had stolen Mrs. Beagle's orange wig. Maggie was in the dream. And Toby. And Mary Reilly. Maggie was his assistant. Toby was the chief of police. Mary Reilly was the criminal. Suddenly Howie was in the newspapers. People were shaking his hand and asking for his autograph. He'd solved the case. Mrs. Beagle had given him a gold star and the principal had invited him over for bean burgers.

Howie woke up. He jumped out of bed. For a second he felt great. Then he looked down. He was in his pajamas. In his new room. He'd been dreaming. Or at least he thought so. But he wasn't sure. What if he really was a secret agent? He smiled to himself.

He put on a pair of wrinkled jeans and a shirt with a small hole in the elbow. Detective Dare Brain always wore something with a hole, for good luck. Then he went down to breakfast.

His mom was at the kitchen sink, squeezing oranges. Dylan was under the table, acting like a dog. "Want some juice, Howie?" asked his mom.

"Don't call me Howie," said Howie. He poured himself a bowl of cereal.

"What did you say?" asked his mom.

"Call me Agent Bean Burger," said Howie confidently.

"Agent Bean Burger?" said his mother. She looked closely at Howie. "Are you feeling all right?" she asked.

"Sure," said Howie.

His mom nodded. "Okay," she said. "How about some juice, then, Agent Bean Burger?" she asked.

"Thank you," said Howie.

His mom poured Howie some juice. Then she spread some mustard on a slice of bread. "Would you mind tossing me an apple, Howie."

"Agent Bean Burger," Howie reminded his mom.

She nodded. "Right," she said. She finished packing Howie's lunch. Then she took a marker and in big bold letters she wrote AGENT BEAN BURGER across the paper bag.

Howie stuffed his books into his knapsack. Along with his Post-Its, colored pencils, a compass, some handcuffs, and his Dare Brain Club membership card. He looked at himself in the toaster and smiled. Was that Howie Bowles? Howie shook his head. He was looking at Secret Agent Bean Burger.

four

Howie sat at his desk chewing on the end of his pencil. Mrs. Beagle was copying multiplication tables on the blackboard. Mary Reilly turned sideways in her seat. She wrinkled up her nose at Howie. Howie wanted to punch her in the face. Or put Double Bubble gum up her nose. But he had to be careful. As a secret agent he couldn't do that. Not until he'd proven she'd committed a crime.

Suddenly Maggie turned around. "Can I borrow your eraser?" she asked. Howie had to think fast. Howie Bowles would have lent her the eraser, no questions asked. But Secret Agent Bean Burger had to be alert.

"What do you want my eraser for?" he asked.

"I made a spelling mistake," said Maggie.

"How do I know you're telling the truth?" asked Howie.

Maggie frowned at Howie.

"My job is to be alert," said Howie. He handed Maggie the pencil.

Maggie erased her mistake. Then she gave the pencil back to Howie. Howie examined it carefully.

"What are you looking for?" asked Maggie. "Germs?"

"Fingerprints," said Howie.

"Huh," said Maggie. She looked puzzled.

Howie shrugged. "That's my job," he said. Howie leaned back in his chair. He pulled out his pad of Post-Its from his desk and a new green pencil. Then he looked carefully around the room. He saw two guys picking their noses, two girls chewing gum, and someone writing on a desk. He was going to be busy.

At lunchtime Howie stood in line at the cafeteria. He'd forgotten his lunch and had to ask Mrs. Beagle for a loan. She'd written his name and the price of a lunch on a note and stuck it under her paperweight. Howie hoped no one saw it. Someone pushed a tray into his back. Howie gazed around doubtfully. He didn't know where the forks were. Or the napkins.

"Hurry up," said a voice. It was Mary Reilly. Howie ignored her and kept moving with the line. Someone shoved a carton of milk in his face. Howie took it and set it on his tray. He dragged his sleeve through his mashed potatoes.

"Brussel sprouts," he mumbled under his breath. That's the word Detective Dare Brain

used when he was upset. He had a clean mouth and was proud of it.

"Who are you talking to?" said someone. Howie looked up. Toby had stopped in front of the desserts and was eating a chocolate brownie.

"I wasn't talking to anyone," said Howie.

"Want a brownie?" asked Toby.

"Sure," said Howie.

"Wait a sec," said Toby. He held the brownie in the air. "How much are you going to pay me for it?" he asked.

Howie reached into his pocket. All he had was five cents.

"I just have a nickel," said Howie.

"No deal," said Toby. He took the brownie back.

"Who's he?" asked the boy in front of Toby.

"He's that new kid I was telling you about," said Mary Reilly, nodding her head toward Howie. She wrinkled up her nose. Then she stretched her mouth into a big round circle. "Howie Bo-o-o-o-owles," she said. She made it sound like Howie's name had five o's. Howie turned around. It was the moment he'd been waiting for.

"How do you know I'm Howie Bowles?" he said.

"What?" said Mary Reilly, wrinkling up her nose again.

"How do you know I'm *really* Howie Bowles," said Howie. "How do you know I'm not a secret agent. Sent by Mr. Mole." Mr. Mole was the school principal.

"A secret agent?" said Toby.

Mary started laughing. "This guy is really strange," she said.

Suddenly a woman's voice came over the loudspeaker. "Agent Bean Burger," she said. "Your lunch is in the office."

Mary looked at Toby. Toby looked at Maggie. Maggie looked at Howie. Howie smiled.

Howie walked into the principal's office.

There was his lunch bag on the counter. AGENT BEAN BURGER was scribbled in big bold letters across the front. Mr. Mole's assistant smiled at Howie. She handed him his lunch. "Your mom dropped this by," she said.

five

Howie looked around the classroom. Someone had left a pencil in the sharpener. Howie wondered who it was. Suddenly Maggie turned around in her seat.

"Are you *really* a secret agent?" she asked.

Howie unzipped his knapsack and pulled out his handcuffs.

"Wow," said Toby. "Do you get paid, too?"

"Sure," said Howie.

Toby offered Howie an Oreo cookie. Free.

"I'd like to get paid for going to school," he said.

Mary Reilly made a face at Howie. "Then what are you doing here?" she asked.

"A lot of crimes happen in the classroom," explained Howie.

"Like what?" asked Mary. She began tapping her foot impatiently. Howie pulled out a Post-It and made a note. Then he nodded.

"Copying, nail-biting, gum chewing," he said. Then he looked straight at Mary Reilly. "And lying," he added. He didn't know why he said that.

Maggie handed Howie her box of Magic Markers. "These are brand-new," she said. "You can use them." She dropped the box on Howie's desk. Howie studied them.

He didn't know what to draw. He chose a blue one and made a large circle. Everyone watched.

Mary went back to her seat. "What's so great about being a secret agent?" she said. She picked up her pencil and began erasing.

"What are you doing?" asked Howie.

"I'm erasing a mistake," said Mary. "Is that a crime?"

"It's getting rid of evidence," said Howie. "I could have you arrested for that." Mary Reilly squirmed in her seat. Howie could see she was worried. Toby laughed.

"What's so funny, fatso?" said Mary Reilly.

"Name-calling is a crime, too," said Howie.

"Huh?" said Mary.

"You shouldn't call people names," said Howie. Mrs. Beagle stood up and clapped her hands.

"I know Howie is new," she said. "And that must be very interesting. But you'll have plenty of time to talk to Howie at recess. Now everyone back to your seats."

At recess Howie began asking questions. A good secret agent was always asking questions.

"Is anything missing from your knapsack?" he asked Toby.

Toby unzipped his knapsack and shook his head. "Just what I've eaten," he said.

Howie picked a pencil up off the pavement. "Does anyone know whose this is?" he asked. No one knew.

Maggie skipped around the side of the building. Howie followed. Someone had written on the wall. M.P. STINKS!

"It's written in red," said Howie, copying his observation down on a Post-It.

"So what?" asked Toby.

Howie quoted Detective Dare Brain. "Color is an important clue," he said. "Are you sure that's red paint?"

"You mean it could be blood?" asked Toby.

"It could be ketchup, too," said Howie matter-of-factly.

Howie walked over to the garbage can and looked inside. "Could someone hand me a stick?" he asked.

Toby handed Howie a stick.

"You never know what could turn up in garbage," said Howie.

Toby stuck his head into the can. "P-U!" he

cried. He poked Howie in the side. "Hey," he said, "what's the hardest case you were ever on?"

Howie had to think fast. "I had to find a marble with a diamond hidden inside," he said. "It was being smuggled out of the country."

"Where did you find it?" asked Toby.

"In the garbage," said Howie. "It was wrapped up in a dirty diaper."

"Gross," said Toby.

"It was my stinkiest case," said Howie.

Toby laughed.

"Who wants to play hopscotch?" someone asked. It was Maggie.

Howie thought he might want to play.

"Naw," said Toby. "Secret agents don't play hopscotch." Toby looked at Howie. Howie thought for a minute. He was confused. But it was a good sort of confused.

"Hmmm," said Howie. He took out a bag of marbles and held it up.

"What's that?" asked Toby. "Some kind of secret weapon?"

Howie shook his head. "Marbles," he said. He lined them up along the pavement. "Want to play?"

Toby rolled a marble across the pavement. Maggie was standing on the hopscotch court, whispering with Mary. She was talking about Secret Agent Bean Burger. She was talking about *him*. Maybe he could hear what she was saying. Howie moved closer. She said he was cute! At least that's what it sounded like.

After school, Howie walked to the corner, where his mother was going to pick him up. He took a deep breath of air. He felt like a new person. Being a secret agent was sure a lot easier than being Howie. Toby admired him. Mary Reilly seemed afraid of him. And Maggie thought he was cute. Howie sighed. Maybe he'd stay a secret agent forever.

six

Howie lay on the carpet. He looked up at the ceiling. Then he stuck his head under a chair.

"Looking for something?" asked his mother.

"Just clues," said Howie. He was practicing being a secret agent.

Howie's mother sat down on the sofa and opened the newspaper. "Was school any better today?" she asked Howie.

"School was fine," said Howie.

"Any new friends?" asked his mother.

Howie nodded. "Yup," he said. Toby was his friend. At least it seemed that way. Actually, Toby was Agent Bean Burger's friend. The thought made Howie feel a little strange. He reached under the chair and pulled out a dime and a piece of half-chewed meat. Howie kept the dime. He handed the meat to his mother.

"What's this?" she asked.

"I think it's Dylan dinner," said Howie. He looked more closely at the meat. "From two weeks ago," he added.

His mom folded up the newspaper. "Dylan," she called.

Howie heard Dylan barking in the kitchen.

"I don't know what I'm going to do with that boy," his mom said. She held up the piece of half-chewed meat. "I need a private eye at mealtimes."

"Then I'm your man," said Howie, shuffling through a stack of old magazines.

His mom nodded knowingly. "So Agent Bean Blooper is still with us," she said.

"That's Burger, Mom," said Howie. "Agent Bean Burger."

"Got you," said his mom. She flipped on the television and turned to the news. "Any idea when we might be seeing Howie again?" she asked.

Howie shook his head. Then he stuffed a pillow under his elbows and stretched out in front of the TV. "Maybe never," he said.

Howie's mother frowned. She looked at the television. Some lady had disappeared off the face of the earth. She had walked into a supermarket and never come out.

Howie's mom shook her head. "What's the world coming to?" she asked.

seven

Howie hurried down to breakfast. His mother was reading a story to Dylan from the back of a cereal box.

"Hey," she said. "Dad called last night. He's got tickets to the Mariners game on Sunday."

"Wow," cried Howie. He'd been dying to go to a Mariners game. "Maybe Ken Griffey will drip mustard on me this time."

"Let's hope so," said his mom. "Dad got an extra ticket, too, if you want to bring a friend."

"A friend?" Howie paused and gulped down his orange juice. "I'll think about it," he said.

Howie sat in the reading circle. Everyone was waiting for Mrs. Beagle. She was talking with another teacher in the corridor.

"I can read upside down," said Mary Reilly. She held up her book and began to read. No one listened.

Toby was doodling with his finger in some chalk dust on the floor. Howie was thinking about the Mariners game on Sunday. He dreamed Ken Griffey launched a high fly ball into the bleachers and he, Howie Bowles, caught it. Howie closed his eyes and imagined the scene.

"Here's your ball, Mr. Griffey," he'd say coolly.

"You can call me Ken," Mr. Griffey would say. "What's your name?"

"Howie Bowles," Howie would say. He'd forgotten all about Agent Bean Burger.

"How about a hot dog after the game?" Mr. Griffey would ask.

"Sure," Howie would say. He'd be wearing his shirt with Ken Griffey ketchup and he'd hold out his arm proudly.

"Wake up!" Mary Reilly kicked Howie's foot. Howie opened his eyes.

Mrs. Beagle came into the room. She looked annoyed. She took her place in the middle of the reading circle.

Suddenly Maggie raised her hand. "Howie's a secret agent," she blurted out. Mrs. Beagle was flipping through the pages of her book. She was only half listening.

"Good," she said. "I need a secret agent. I'd like to know who's putting gum in the water fountains." Mrs. Beagle looked up from her book. "It's a crime."

Howie glanced around. Everyone was looking at him.

Toby stopped doodling. "Howie's your man," he said.

"I am?" said Howie. Then he remembered.

He was Secret Agent Bean Burger. "I am," he said firmly.

Mrs. Beagle nodded and began reading aloud. Howie had a hard time concentrating. He kept thinking about the water fountains. Someone was putting gum in them. And he had to find out who.

At recess Howie spotted a gum wrapper on the ground. He picked it up and stuffed it into his pocket.

"What's that?" asked Toby.

"Evidence," said Howie. He sat down on the steps. Mary galloped by. She was chewing gum. Howie sniffed. Strawberry Tingle. He pulled out his pencil and a Post-It. He'd have to make a note of that.

Howie followed Toby to the hopscotch court. Maggie was standing on the number 2 square. A wad of gum was stuck on the number 3 square. Orange gum. Howie leaned over for a closer look.

"Got any ideas?" asked Toby.

Howie traced a large circle around the gum with a piece of chalk.

"Do you know who did it?" asked Maggie.

"Everyone's a suspect," said Howie.

"Everyone?" said Maggie. She looked worried. So Howie added, "But you're all innocent until proven guilty." Maggie looked relieved. She took three jumps forward. Howie wondered if she'd ask him to play. She didn't.

Howie felt Toby's elbow in his rib. "If you want, I'll be your assistant," he said. "For free."

"Okay," said Howie. Toby led Howie over to the monkey bars.

"Take a look at this," said Toby. The ground under the monkey bars was covered with gum.

Howie pulled out another Post-It and began taking notes. The criminal may have been on the monkey bars. That made Howie think of something. Maggie was always on the monkey bars. Maybe that was her gum on the ground. Maybe she was putting gum in the water fountains. It seemed unlikely, but it was possible.

Anything was possible. If it was Maggie, he'd have to turn her in. She might get kicked out of school. And it would be all his fault. Actually, it would be her fault. He was just doing his job. Still, the thought bothered Howie. Howie looked over at the tetherball. He thought he'd like to play.

"Want to play?" asked Myron.

"He can't," answered Toby. "He's on a case."

"Quiet," said Howie. "You want the whole school to know?"

"Sorry," whispered Toby. "I won't tell anyone." But by noon everyone knew that Howie Bowles was Secret Agent Bean Burger on a very important case.

eight

Howie spent the rest of the day drinking water. There were four water fountains in Palmer Elementary. One outside the office, one outside Mrs. Beagle's room, and two beside the bathrooms.

"We've got to check them all," Howie said to Toby at recess. Two of them had gum stuck to the spout. Green gum. Howie took out a Post-It. He began writing. *Watch out for green-gum chewers.* He'd have to keep his eyes open. Green-gum chewers were prime suspects.

"Are we going to take fingerprints?" asked Toby.

Detective Dare Brain used fingerprints to solve a case when there were only a few suspects. There were two hundred kids at Palmer Elementary. Besides, fingerprints wouldn't help much.

"We need toothprints," said Howie. All chewed gum had toothprints.

"How are we going to get those?" asked Toby.

"I don't know," said Howie.

"Look," cried Toby. He'd spotted a fourth-grader chomping on something.

"We're going to have to check that out," said Howie. He marched up to the fourth-grader.

"Ah, excuse me, sir," he said. Detective Dare Brain was always polite. Even when talking to a suspect.

"My name's not sir," said the guy. "It's Jason."

"Mind if I ask you a few questions, Jason?" said Howie. He took out his pencil and a Post-It.

"Sure I do, squirt," said Jason. Then he blew a huge bubble in Howie's face.

"You know who you're talking to?" said Toby. "This is Agent Bean Burger."

Jason looked at Howie. He started laughing. "And I'm the King of England," he said. "Get lost."

Howie thought they'd better take Jason's advice. It seemed safer.

"Gee," said Howie. "You can sure make a lot of enemies in this line of work." Detective Dare Brain had forgotten to mention that.

Howie stepped onto the basketball court.

"Watch out," cried someone. Suddenly a ball banged against Howie's nose. It hurt. Howie sat down on a bench. Toby sat beside him.

"You think I could be a detective someday?" he asked. "I can smell a piece of chocolate fifty feet away."

Howie couldn't smell anything. His nose was all stuffed up. "Why not?" he said. "I mean, if you really want to be." Howie was beginning to think it wasn't such a great idea.

"Too bad," said Toby.

"What's too bad?" asked Howie.

"I guess you'll be leaving," said Toby.

Howie sunk his teeth into the end of his pencil. "Huh?" he said.

"After this case is over," said Toby.

Howie hadn't thought about it, but Toby was right. He couldn't stay on the case forever. What kind of a secret agent would he be?

Toby opened a pack of Life Savers. He offered one to Howie. "My dog is lost," he said. "He's been lost for five days. Maybe you could find him."

"Me?" said Howie.

"Sure," said Toby. "I'll even pay you. Three dollars and fifty cents."

"You don't have to pay me," said Howie.

"I could bring a picture of my dog over to your office," said Toby. "That way, you'd know what he looks like."

"Office?" said Howie. Of course, if he was a secret agent, he'd have to have an office.

"Or I could bring it by your house," said Toby.

"No!" cried Howie. He couldn't have Toby come to his house. He'd find out that Howie had parents. That he had a brother named Dylan who thought he was a dog. He'd find out that Howie wasn't really a secret agent.

"His name is Fritz," said Toby.

"Nice name," said Howie. He didn't know what else to say.

"Want to ask me some questions?" asked Toby.

Howie did want to ask Toby a question. He wanted to ask Toby if he liked baseball. Instead, he asked Toby if his dog had a collar.

nine

Howie dove onto the floor beside Dylan. Dylan was watching his favorite cartoon on TV.

Dylan handed Howie a piece of crumpled-up newspaper. "Can you make a boat?" he said. Howie made great boats out of newspaper.

"What do you say?" said Howie.

"Please," said Dylan.

"All right," said Howie. Howie folded Dylan a boat. "How's that?" he asked. Dylan smiled.

Howie took another piece of paper and folded another boat. "We could make a whole fleet," he said.

"What's a fleet?" asked Dylan.

"A fleet is a lot of boats that sail together," explained Howie. "I'll be the captain and you can be first mate."

"Okay," said Dylan. He sailed his boat under the table. It got stuck on a chair.

"Help, Mr. Bean Burger!" cried Dylan.

"It's Agent Bean Burger," said Howie.

Howie ducked under the table. The phone rang.

"Answer it, Dylan," called Howie.

Dylan answered the phone. "It's Daddy," he said. Howie listened to Dylan explain how he'd made a duck in school. A yellow duck. Then he heard Dylan say, "Howie isn't here."

"Yes I am," cried Howie from under the table.

Howie yanked the phone out of Dylan's hand. "Why did you say I wasn't here?"

"Howie doesn't live here anymore," said Dylan. "Agent Bean Burger lives here."

Howie looked at Dylan. Maybe Dylan was right. Howie didn't live here anymore. The thought made Howie feel strange.

"Is that you, How?" asked his dad.

"Yup," said Howie. He looked for the mole on his right arm just to be sure.

"Are you all set for the game on Sunday?" asked his dad.

"You bet," said Howie. "Let's hope it doesn't rain."

"That would be a crime," said his dad.

Howie nodded silently. Even rain had become a crime.

"Be good," said Howie's dad. "See you on Friday."

"Bye, Dad," said Howie. He put down the receiver and looked at the television.

"What we need are more law-enforcement officials," a man was saying.

Howie nodded. That made him feel a little

better. Then he flipped to another station. A girl was singing. She looked just like Maggie, only fatter. Howie wondered if it could be her sister. Or maybe a cousin or an aunt. He'd ask her.

ten

The rest of the week was a blur. On Thursday, Mrs. Beagle chose a class monitor. She picked Myron.

"I'm going to be class monitor next," said Mary Reilly. "For a whole month," she added.

"Good for you," said Toby. He pointed to Howie. "This guy's a secret agent. That's like being a class monitor for life."

Howie looked over at Mary Reilly. She was passing notes. That was against the rules. He could say something. But today he didn't feel like it. Today he felt tired. Besides, Mary Reilly's mother was on the school board. That was like being President of the United States. She could do anything. The thought made Howie nervous.

Howie sighed. The case wasn't going well. He'd been drinking water all week. And he'd counted sixty-four pieces of chewed-up gum. Still he had no idea who was putting gum in the water fountains. Worse, he wasn't sure he wanted to know. Howie slid lower in his chair. He was beginning to wonder if it wouldn't be easier just being Howie.

Howie looked at the blackboard. Mrs. Beagle was looking at him oddly. Come to think of it, she'd been looking at him oddly a lot lately. Like *he'd* committed some kind of crime. That afternoon, Mrs. Beagle called on Howie for the first time. Howie hadn't done his arithmetic homework. He'd been too busy writing down questions for suspects.

"Didn't you do your homework, Howie?" Mrs. Beagle wanted to know.

"Sort of," said Howie. After all, he had stayed up until eleven studying Detective Dare Brain's crime manual. He just hadn't done his arithmetic. It was hard being a detective and a third-grader at the same time. Didn't Mrs. Beagle realize that?

That night, Howie dreamed he was arrested. He was arrested by Secret Agent Bean Burger on two counts. For lying and for assuming a false identity. He had to pay a fine of twenty-five brownies. Howie woke up feeling tired.

eleven

Howie watched Mrs. Beagle climb onto a chair. She reached for something in the cupboard above her desk. Her slip was showing. That was embarrassing. Howie looked down at his pants. He checked to make sure his fly was zipped. Maggie got up to sharpen her pencil. That reminded Howie of the show he'd seen on television and the singer who looked like Maggie.

Maggie sat down in her seat. Howie kicked the back of her chair. "Do you have any sisters?" he asked.

Maggie frowned. "Why do you want to know?" she said. "Is it a crime to have sisters?"

"I saw a woman on TV," said Howie. "She looked like you. I thought maybe it was your sister. Or a cousin or something."

Maggie shook her head. "I don't know anyone on television," she said.

Howie was still curious. He still wondered if Maggie had any sisters. He wondered where she lived. He wondered what color her house was.

"What color is your house?" asked Howie.

"Why are you asking?" said Maggie.

"I was just wondering," said Howie.

Maggie shook her head. "I'd rather not say," she said.

"All right," said Howie. He shrugged. After all, Maggie was right. You had to be careful when you talked to a secret agent. Anything you said could be used against you.

Howie went back to his arithmetic problems. He heard a funny noise next to him.

Mary Reilly was clicking her tongue against the roof of her mouth. Then she began stretching her mouth in a dozen different directions. Maybe she was trying to tell him something. The thought made Howie uncomfortable. He fidgeted in his chair. He couldn't wait until school was over.

After school, Howie stopped by the boys' room. He had to go to the bathroom. He had to go to the bathroom a lot lately. That's because he was drinking so much water.

He stood before the bathroom mirror and looked at himself. He looked tired. And he looked different. He didn't look like himself. Maybe he was really becoming another person. Howie panicked. He thought about Agent Bean Burger. What if he did solve the case? He'd have to turn the criminal in, even if it was Maggie or Toby. Or he'd have to turn himself in. Howie sighed. Maybe he could just stay here in the bathroom forever.

Just then, Howie heard footsteps. Someone

was coming down the corridor. The bathroom door swung open. Mary Reilly stood in front of Howie, tapping her foot.

"Girls aren't allowed in the boys' bathroom," said Howie. His voice had begun to squeak.

"Then why don't you arrest me?" said Mary. She made a face at Howie. Howie squirmed.

"Guess what?" said Mary.

"Your mother's on the school board," said Howie quickly.

Mary Reilly nodded. "And she knows everything about everybody in this school," said Mary.

"She does?" said Howie. He tried to smile, but his mouth felt stiff.

Mary Reilly smiled. She knew. Mary Reilly knew that Howie wasn't really a secret agent. Howie knew she knew. For a second Howie felt relieved. And then he panicked. He had to pee.

"Excuse me," he said. And he ducked into a stall. He could still hear Mary Reilly tapping her foot against the floor. She tapped for thirty whole seconds and then Howie heard the bathroom door swing shut.

twelve

Howie slunk home from school. He jumped at the sound of passing cars. He wondered if Mary Reilly was hiding in the bushes waiting to pounce. She was probably home preparing a huge note to the class. "Howie Bowles is a liar," it would say. Lying was a classroom crime. Maybe he'd get kicked out of school. Maybe he shouldn't bother returning to school. Then he wouldn't have to face the class. But he'd have to go back to school sometime. He couldn't stay out of school for the rest of his life. He'd grow up stupid.

Dylan was waiting for Howie in the front yard. He was down on his hands and knees, with his head in the bushes.

"Dylan," cried Howie. "Please stop acting like a dog."

"Help, Agent Burger," said Dylan. "I've lost my ball."

Howie got down on his hands and knees. "It's Howie," he said. "My name is Howie. Agent Bean Burger's been picked off by a snoop."

"What's a snoop?" asked Dylan.

"A spy," said Howie. He poked his head under a bush and pulled out Dylan's ball. "Here," he said.

"Thank you," said Dylan. He kicked the ball and it rolled under the bush again.

Howie's mother was in the kitchen, unpacking groceries. "I got some more ketchup," she said. "We can make bean burgers this week-end."

Howie felt his stomach turn. He reached into his knapsack and pulled out his Post-Its. Twenty-seven of them filled with Agent Bean Burger's notes.

"What's that?" asked his mother.

"Homework," said Howie.

"Since when do you do homework on Post-Its?" his mother wanted to know.

Howie didn't have a chance to answer. The phone rang.

"Would you get that, Howie?" asked his mother.

Howie picked up the phone. It was for his mother. "Could I ask who's calling, please?"

"Phyllis Reilly," said the woman on the other end of the phone. Howie froze. It was Mary Reilly's mother, president of the school board. And she wanted to speak to Howie's mother.

"She's busy right now," said Howie. "Why don't you call back next week. Or next year," he added.

Howie's mother reached for the phone. "What's gotten into you?" she said. Then she took one of Howie's Post-Its and began scribbling. When she hung up she frowned at Howie. "That was Phyllis Reilly," she said. "She wants to see me."

"She does?" said Howie. His voice sounded far away.

"Urgent school-board business," said Howie's mother.

Howie tried to breathe deeply. Even if Mary's mother was president of the school board, there was only so much she could do. Maybe she could get Howie kicked out of school, but she couldn't send him to jail.

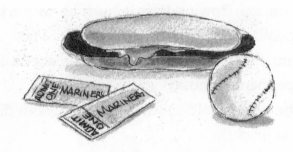

thirteen

Howie dragged himself to school. He took his
seat in the third row just like always. In front
of him, Maggie was twisting her finger around
a curl. Toby was folding a candy-bar wrapper
into a paper jet. Howie looked to his right.
Mary Reilly's desk was empty. Howie looked at
the clock. It was past nine. Mary wasn't coming. She was absent. Howie felt his body tingle. Mary Reilly was absent. That meant she
was sick. Maybe she'd be sick for the rest of

the year. Or maybe she had to move unexpect-
edly. Wouldn't that be great. Howie settled into
his seat and began copying spelling words off
the board. "Plight, tight, white, sight." He had
just finished writing "sight" when Mary Reilly
skipped into the room. She handed Mrs.
Beagle a note. Then she took her seat. She
smiled brightly.

"I've come from the dentist," she said. "No
cavities."

"Congratulations," said Toby. He handed
Mary an empty lollypop stick.

Mary Reilly glared at Howie. "Today is show
and *tell*," she said.

Howie glanced quickly around the room. He
looked for somewhere he could hide when
Mary Reilly stood up and told the entire
class that he wasn't a secret agent. That there
was no case. That there was no Agent Bean
Burger.

Howie stared at his spelling words.

"I'm in a terrible plight," he thought. "I wish

I were out of sight. My shoes feel tight." Howie began to sweat. His mouth was dry. He needed a drink of water.

Howie raised his hand. "May I get a drink of water, Mrs. Beagle?" he asked.

"You should have done that earlier," said Mrs. Beagle. But she let him go.

Howie started into the corridor. There was Mr. Mole, the principal, coming down the hall. Howie panicked. Maybe Mary had already told Mr. Mole and Mr. Mole was coming to get him. Howie ducked into an empty classroom. Mr. Mole stopped in front of the drinking fountain and scratched his balding head. He was only getting a drink. Howie could see Mr. Mole's mouth moving. He was talking to someone. Howie stretched his neck to see who was there. No one was there. Mr. Mole was talking to himself. No. He was chewing gum! Mr. Mole, the principal, was chewing gum. That was against the rules. Mr. Mole bent over to get a drink. He took three sips of water. Then

he stood up. He stopped chewing. Where was his gum? He had either swallowed it, which was gross, or he'd gotten rid of it.

Howie stepped up to the drinking fountain. Mr. Mole tacked a notice to the bulletin board in the hallway and returned to his office. Howie bent over for a drink. There was a big fat wad of gum stuck to the water fountain. Green gum. Howie touched it.

"It's still fresh," he said. "And warm." Howie wrinkled his nose like Mary Reilly. Then he pursed his lips like Detective Dare Brain.

Mrs. Beagle peeked into the corridor. Howie could see Mary Reilly poking her big nose around the corner.

"Is there a problem, Howie?" asked Mrs. Beagle.

Howie stepped back into the classroom. He looked at Mary. Now was his chance.

He cleared his voice. Detective Dare Brain always cleared his voice before making an important statement. "I believe I know who's putting gum in the water fountains," said Howie.

"You mean you've solved the case," said Toby. "Way to go. Who is it?"

"It's whom you may have least suspected," said Howie. "As often is the case." Howie sighed. "It's Mr. Mole, the principal," he said.

Mrs. Beagle raised her eyebrows. Toby burst out laughing. And Mary Reilly stretched her mouth into a big wide O.

"Are you sure about that, Howie?" asked Mrs. Beagle.

"Sure he's sure," said Toby. "Agent Bean Burger never utters a word without being one hundred percent certain."

"That's true," said Howie.

"Aren't you going to arrest him?" Maggie wanted to know.

"I'll arrest him," said Toby.

"I think we'd better leave that to Agent Bean Burger," said Mrs. Beagle. She clapped her hands. "Now everyone back to their seats."

Howie sat down. He smiled to himself. He had solved a crime. He could go on being Secret Agent Bean Burger for the rest of his life. The only trouble was, he didn't want to. Suddenly he remembered what Mrs. Beagle had said. Did she really believe he was a secret agent? Did she really expect him to arrest Mr. Mole? He was the principal. He was the one in charge.

Howie picked up his pencil. His hands felt clammy. He finished copying the spelling words off the board.

"Howie," said Mrs. Beagle. She wanted to see him at her desk.

Howie walked up to Mrs. Beagle's desk. "Is there something you want to say to me?" she asked. There was something Howie wanted to say. He thought he might as well say it.

"Were you born with that hair?" asked Howie. Mrs. Beagle raised her eyebrows. And she smiled.

"No," she said. "I wasn't. I color it. It's brown underneath."

"Oh," said Howie. He wondered what was next.

Mrs. Beagle just kept looking at him. At last she said, "Can I ask you a question?"

"Sure," said Howie. "Teachers can do whatever they want."

"Teachers have rules, too," said Mrs. Beagle. "And principals as well," she added. "Would you like me to speak to Mr. Mole about the gum?"

Howie couldn't believe his ears. "Would you mind?" he said.

"Not at all," said Mrs. Beagle. "But I think arrest might be too strong of a punishment. I'll have to think of something a little less severe."

"Gee, thanks," said Howie. "That would be great."

Mrs. Beagle shuffled through some papers on her desk. "I know you must be very busy, Agent Bean Burger," she said. Howie couldn't figure out if she was smiling or not. "Still," she added, "now that you've solved this case, I was wondering if you'd like to start work on a new one."

"A new case?" asked Howie. The idea terrified him.

Mrs. Beagle nodded. "Yes," she said. "A very important case."

Howie looked for the fire exit. Was there no way out?

Mrs. Beagle picked up her attendance chart. "I was hoping you could help me find a missing person," she said.

"A missing person?" Howie asked.

"I'm looking for Howie Bowles," said Mrs. Beagle. "The real Howie Bowles. The boy who's supposed to be in my classroom." Mrs. Beagle smiled at Howie. Howie smiled back. She knew and she understood.

Howie nodded. He turned to go back to his seat. Toby was gazing out of the window. He winked at Howie. Howie winked back.

"So what's next, Bean Burger?" he asked.

"I think I'm going to take a little vacation,"

said Howie. "This private-eye stuff can be pretty tiring. I thought I might catch a baseball game."

"Baseball?" said Toby.

"Sure," said Howie. "I've got an extra ticket to the Mariners game. Want to come?"

"Great!" said Toby. "My mouth is watering already. Baseball and hot dogs."

Howie sat down. He remembered what his mother had said. "Don't worry. Just be yourself." Howie began to worry. That was being himself. He was a worrier. Howie picked up his pencil. He wrote his name across the top of his paper. "Howie Bowles," he said aloud.

He looked down at his feet. Suddenly he started laughing.

"What are you laughing at?" demanded Mary Reilly.

Howie looked at Mary's feet. "What if your feet started growing?" he asked. "What if they grew to be bigger than your body."

"You're weird," said Mary Reilly.

"It could happen," said Howie. "Anything could happen." Suddenly Mary looked worried. She looked down at her feet.

Pretty soon everybody was looking at their feet. Howie laughed again. This time it wasn't because he was nervous. He just felt like laughing and everyone laughed with him.